Sam Squeak and the Man on the Tree

Joseph Zmuda

Illustrated Trinity Shubin

Edited by Matt Blount

Email: SamSqueakBook@gmail.com

ISBN: 9781095331347

DEDICATION

To the loves of my life, My Lord God, my wife and my children.
Special Thank you to Pastor Jeri Houle, without her encouragement this would be just a fun story.

Sam Squeak
and the Man
On the Tree

By Joseph Zmuda

Illustrated by Trinity Shubin

Hi! I'm Sam, Sam Squeak, I'm a jerboa mouse. I spend most of my days sleeping in this nice little cave (that some guy named Joseph dug out), and most nights searching for food and other things I need. But this last week it has been weird. I have been awake more days and not getting much rest.

I try to stay away from people for the most part, being that most of the time if I'm seen then there is screaming and yelling and sometimes even knives. One of my cousins lost half his tail… but that is a story for another time.

This time-of-year is the best, it's a feast; so many people and so many things to eat. With everyone in town for one of these great feasts here in Jerusalem things are great; so much food more food than you could imagine eating in a lifetime…well maybe you but certainly not little me.

So, a few days ago everyone started showing up and getting ready for this great feast. Of course, I'm ready to eat everything I can find; bread, fish, lamb, and the drinks they would bring - WOW so good!

A few days ago, I guess everyone is getting ready. I was sleeping in my cool cave. This great earth shake woke me up and I ran out to look around. To my surprise the sun had disappeared. With it dark out I went exploring.

I found myself in a disgusting place where these Roman guards were playing dice to see who gets to take some clothes home. I guess they used to belong to one of those guys hung up on those odd trees. As I was getting ready to head back to the town to find some more food I heard this man who was on one of those trees say, "It is Finished," whatever that meant.

I made my way through town and I went to the Temple. There's always bread and grain around there that I can snack on. When I get there, everyone is going crazy and this time it is not because of me. This big cloth they had hanging up was torn in two, and I heard someone say it was split from the top down. I thought, "Who would have climbed all the way up there to cut it that way?" With everyone so crazy it was easy to get some food and make my way back to the cave.

As I got back to my cave there was a huge rock put in front of it and some of those Roman guys were there too. That Joseph guy must have found out that I had been staying there and didn't want me to stay anymore. Not knowing where to go, I decided not to go too far. I found a small hole near the cave and was going to stay there for a bit until I found something better.

Now that it has been a couple of days, it is nice having these guards here watching over my old cave because they are messy eaters… so I don't really have to go anywhere to get food. It's been great!

So, Sunday morning came very early for most humans and starting to get late for me, I heard this loud noise and saw this magnificent light shining near that great rock they put in front of my cave, and those guards just fell over like they died on their feet or something.

Then that light pushed the rock out of the way and out of my cave walked that guy from the tree. Now he is aglow - shining brighter than anything I had ever seen before. Even the sun looked dim. He stepped out and stretched like he had just woken up from a nap.

Then I hear these ladies come from up the street. They were crying and talking about some Jesus guy… was that the guy from the tree? As they got close enough to see the rock was moved they freaked out say things like, "Who took him?" and "Give him back to us!"

Then the light turned to them and said, "Do not be afraid, for I know that you seek Jesus whom was crucified. He is not here, for He is Risen, just as He said. Come; see the place where He lay. Then go quickly and tell the disciples that He is risen from the dead, and behold, He is going before you to Galilee; there you will see Him." At this these ladies got so happy and ran off. Then the light left.

I was glad of the quiet for a bit and hopeful to get my cave back. Then these two guys come running up and one of them ran right into my cave and started looking around at the stuff that this Jesus guy left in there. I thought it was going to make a great bed but not my luck. After all this commotion I think I really need to find another place to stay.

ABOUT THE AUTHOR

Joseph Zmuda is a tattooed, pierced, motorcycle riding follower of the most high God. He has a BA in Leadership and Ministry from Multnomah University in Portland Oregon. Joseph has a wife and 2 children, and is teaching where and when the Lord God leads.

Made in the USA
Middletown, DE
08 September 2020